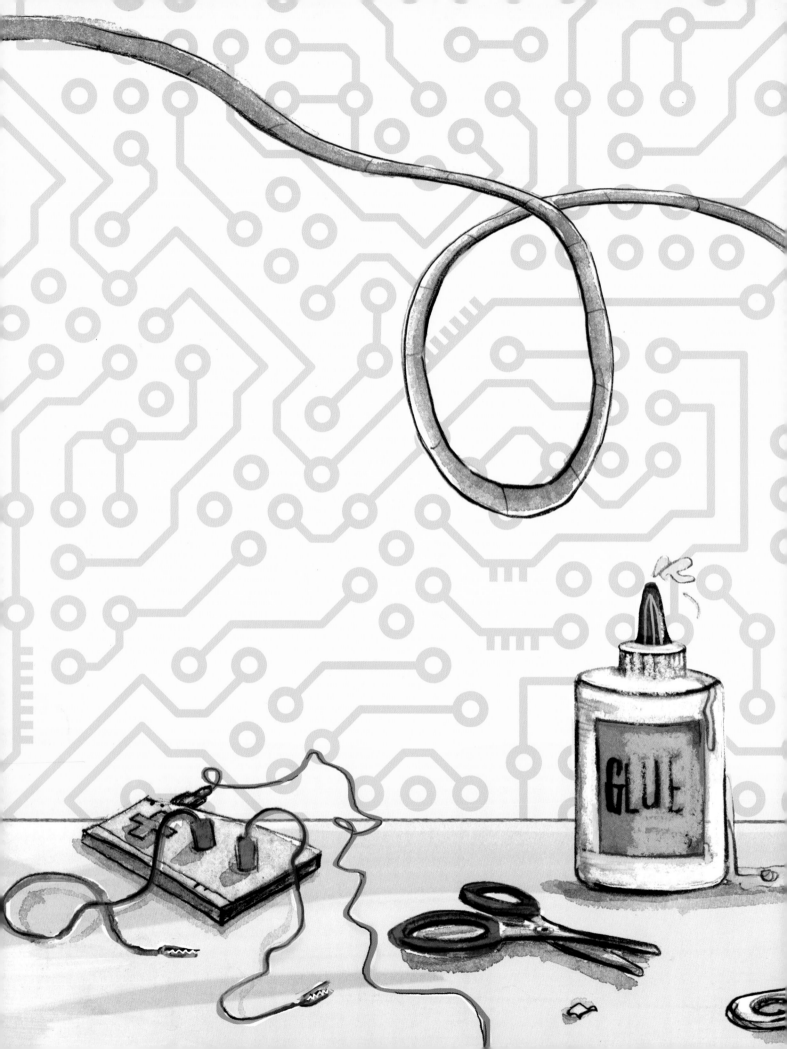

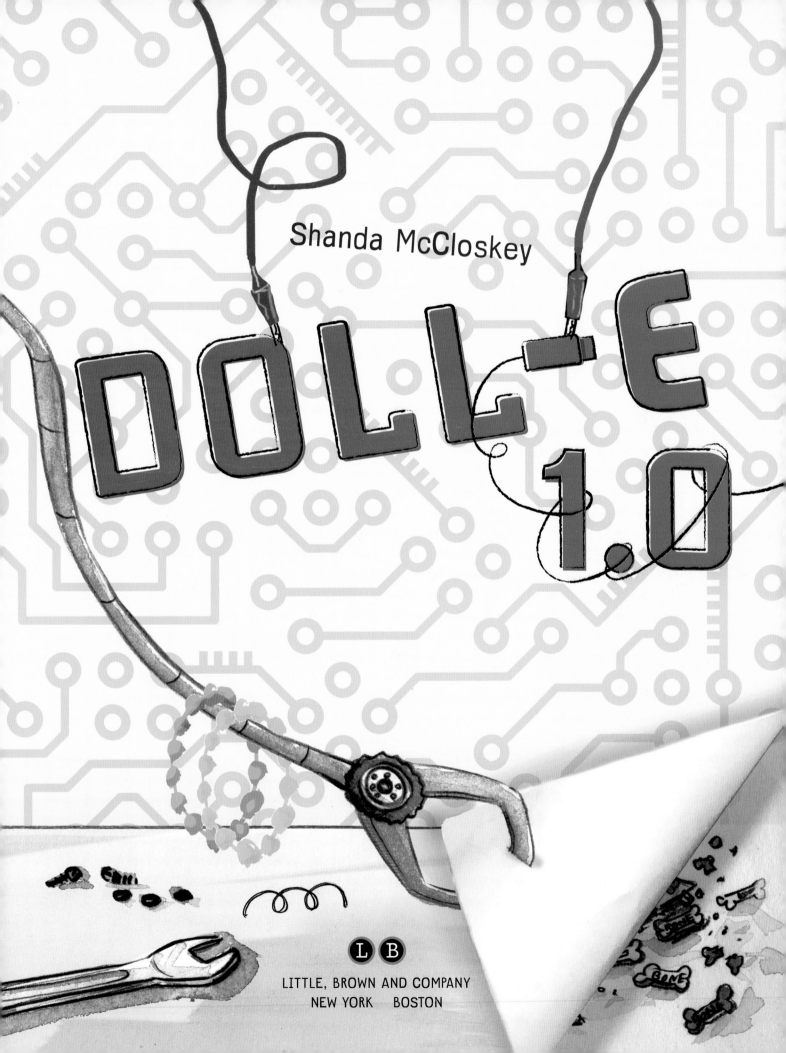

Shanda McCloskey

DOLL-E 1.0

L B

LITTLE, BROWN AND COMPANY

NEW YORK   BOSTON

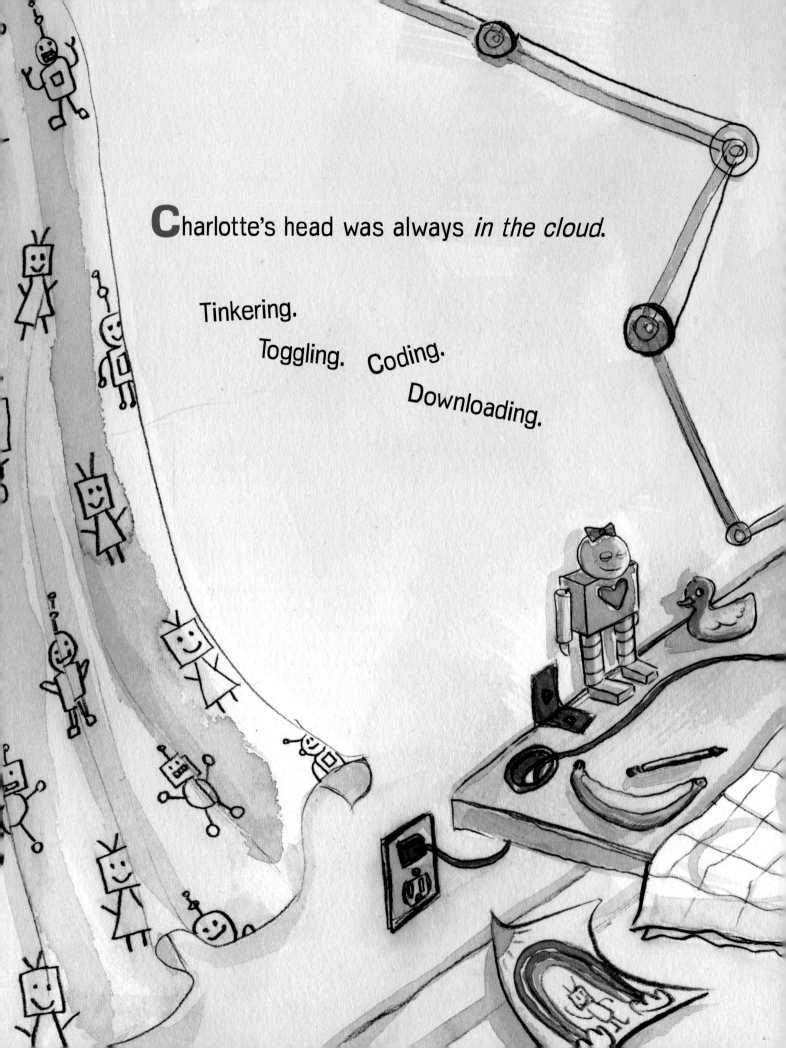

Charlotte's head was always *in the cloud.*

Tinkering.

Toggling. Coding.

Downloading.

She was Mama's little genius.

And Daddy's little smarty-pants.

Charlotte's world was fully charged!

One day, Mama had a present for Charlotte.

Is it a dog-bark decoder device so I can know what Blutooth is saying?!

Nope. Even better!

Charlotte dragged the human-shaped pillow to her room.

She tried sharing her spare-parts collection.

She even tried a dance party.

But the doll just . . .

Then Charlotte thought of something.
If the doll could talk, then it must have a . . .

Now things were getting interesting.

Charlotte couldn't let it end this way.

She knew what she had to do.

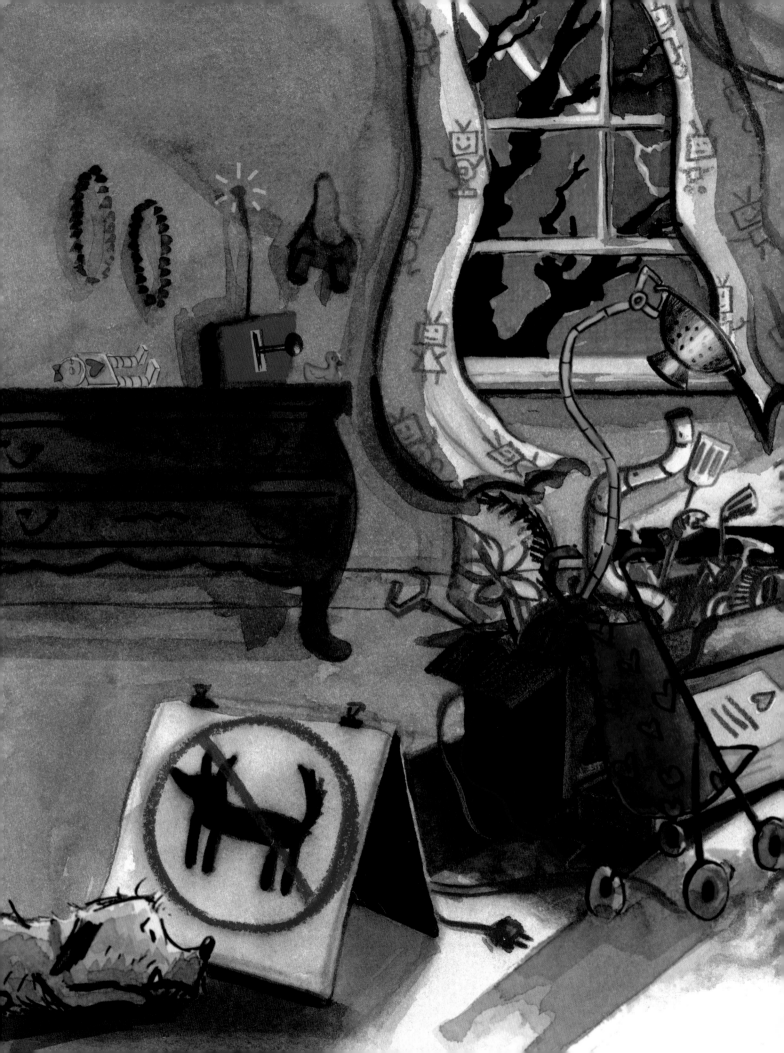

With a few spare parts and a bit of code, Charlotte changed the doll.

With two bright eyes and a cute little battery pack . . .

Doll-E, wanna take Blutooth for a walk with . . . Mama?

. . . the doll changed Charlotte, too.

For Ben, Harvey Jane, Beni, Jovie, and Dusty (the robot vacuum)

ABOUT THIS BOOK: The illustrations for this book were drawn in pencil, painted in watercolor, and then edited in Photoshop. This book was edited by Andrea Spooner and designed by Jen Keenan. The production was supervised by Erika Schwartz, and the production editor was Jen Graham. The text was set in Imperfect and Zemke Hand ITC.

 • Little, Brown and Company • Hachette Book Group • 1290 Avenue of the Americas, New York, NY 10104 • Visit us at LBYR.com • First Edition: May 2018 • Little, Brown and Company is a division of Hachette Book Group, Inc. The Little, Brown name and logo are trademarks of Hachette Book Group, Inc. • The publisher is not responsible for websites (or their content) that are not owned by the publisher. • Library of Congress Cataloging-in-Publication Data • Names: McCloskey, Shanda, author, illustrator. • Title: Doll-E 1.0 / Shanda McCloskey. • Description: First Edition. | New York : Little, Brown and Company, 2018. | Summary: Charlotte has a talent for anything technological, so when she receives a doll as a present, she upgrades it with a few spare parts and some code to create a new and improved friend. • Identifiers: LCCN 2017012824| ISBN 9780316510318 (hardcover) | ISBN 9780316510325 (ebook) | ISBN 9780316510301 (library edition ebook) • Subjects: | CYAC: Dolls—Fiction. | Technology—Fiction. • Classification: LCC PZ7.1.M42215 Do 2018 | DDC [E]—dc23 • LC record available at https://lccn.loc.gov/2017012824 • ISBNs: 978-0-316-51031-8 (hardcover), 978-0-316-51032-5 (ebook), 978-0-316-51029-5 (ebook), 978-0-316-51033-2 (ebook) • PRINTED IN CHINA • 1010 • 10 9 8 7 6 5